To Hannah, Joseph, Daniel, Rosie and Emily
K. K. & S. N.

To Ben
C. C.

First edition for the United States published 1991
by Barron's Educational Series, Inc.

Originally published by J.M. Dent and Sons, Ltd, London, 1991.

Text copyright © Kate Khdir and Sue Nash, 1991.

Illustrations copyright © Caroline Church, 1991.

All inquiries should be addressed to:
Barron's Educational Series, Inc.
250 Wireless Boulevard
Hauppauge, New York 11788

International Standard Book No. 0–8120–4779–6

Library of Congress Catalog Card No. 90–43178

Library of Congress Cataloging-in-Publication Data

Khdir, Kate.
    Little ghost/by Kate Khdir and Sue Nash: illustrated by Caroline Church.

    p.   cm.
    Summary: Ghost's attempts to scare the pupils at a human school result in his becoming part of
their Halloween play.
    ISBN 0–8120–4779–6
    [1. Ghosts—Fiction. 2. Schools—Fiction, 3. Halloween—Fiction.] I. Nash. Sue. II. Church,
Caroline, III, III. Title. PZ7. K5266Li 1991
[E]—dc20

90–43178
CIP
AC

PRINTED IN ITALY

1234 987654321

Little Ghost

by Kate Khdir and Sue Nash

Illustrated by Caroline Church

BARRON'S
New York

On a quiet street, among ordinary houses like yours and mine, stood a large, empty, spooky house.

Everything was rundown inside, but perfect as far as the Principal, Miss Scarum, was concerned. It had creepy cobwebs, huge, hairy spiders, creaky doors, and dust thick enough to write your name in. In fact, it had every modern convenience a spook could want.

SCHOOL
for Ghosts
and Ghouls

Principal:
Miss I Scarum

"You've all done very well in your scaring tests," said Miss Scarum to her class. "All except you, Little Ghost." "You've been a very silly little ghost," she snapped. "Today is your last chance. You'd better scare somebody or you'll have to stay down with the babies next term."

The bell rang and everyone rushed outside screeching and whooping. Little Ghost trailed after them.

"Perhaps you should go to the human school down the road," Miss Scarum muttered. "Those stuffy human teachers could do with a fright, and even *you* should be able to scare children."

Little Ghost wasn't sure about that. Children were such a noisy group he was a bit scared of them.

He reached the playground and watched the children going into school. Gathering up his courage he floated in through the closed door.

He followed the sound of voices and found himself behind some thick red curtains. From the other side someone was saying, "This afternoon we're having our school play, *The Halloween Party*. Would the witches go for a hat fitting in the sewing room, please. Everyone else, back to class!"

Little Ghost saw his big chance – a whole school to terrify!
He leaped through the curtains, waving his arms. Quietly the
children filed out. Nobody screamed . . . nobody even noticed!
  "They're brave," thought Little Ghost. Then he realized he
had forgotten to make himself visible.

He floated down a corridor peeping through doors. He spied some children sloshing around with paint and big brushes.

"If I scare them, there will be a terrible mess," he chuckled.

But then a little girl shouted, "I'm going to paint a big star for the wizard's cloak."

Little Ghost felt a wet tickly feeling between his shoulders. She had painted a huge star across his back.

"Oh, dear," he sighed, and slid through the nearest wall.

He looked around. He seemed to be in the bathroom. "How lucky," he thought. "I can wash off this awful star." Suddenly, two boys rushed through the door, turned on the faucets, and splashed water at each other. They dried their hands and ran out laughing. Little Ghost looked down at his tummy which was covered with black handprints. "What nerve! They think I'm a towel," he wailed.

"I mustn't give up. I must be brave," he decided, and marched through the wall. To his surprise, he was surrounded by whirring and buzzing machines. There was dress material everywhere. Little Ghost was in the sewing room.

"Quick! Pass me that material so I can make the last ghost costume."

A hand grabbed him and he was slapped down hard on a table. A machine rattled, and he felt little pricks down one side. He was flipped over and was sewn down the other side. (Luckily you can't hurt a ghost!)

A bell rang and all the children went out. Everything was quiet.

Little Ghost disentangled himself, unpopped the stitches, and said, "This is silly. I *must* pass my test."

Before he knew it he had floated into the lunchroom.

"Hello, ghostie," said a little boy. "You're in your costume early. What are *you* eating —, batburgers and spookghetti?" Everyone giggled but Little Ghost just stared at his plate. "Little Ghosts don't eat," he said in a very small voice.

Everyone giggled again. Then they gobbled up their food and went to put their costumes on.

"I give up. I'll never be able to scare anyone," Little Ghost thought. He drifted behind the curtains onto the stage again. Everything looked different. Little Ghost climbed onto the high black chair in the center of the stage.

Suddenly, loud music started, the curtains swept open and little witches, wizards, and a crowd of ghostly figures ran on from all sides, shrieking.

Little Ghost was so surprised that he shot up into the air.
"Marvelous! Bravo! What a trick!" shouted the
audience. He flitted through a scenery wall.
"Amazing! How did he do that?" the children whispered.
"Go back on," a teacher hissed, giving him a gentle push.

Little Ghost glided back through the scenery. Everyone gasped in disbelief.

"What a wonderful ghost!" the audience exclaimed. Little Ghost blushed with pride. He was the star of the show.

After the clapping had finished, Little Ghost rushed back to Miss Scarum's. She was in the classroom teaching the spooks a difficult spell.

"Eye of toad, wing of bat," she sang.

Little Ghost burst in and shrieked, "I'm famous!"

"Creeping cobwebs!" screeched Miss Scarum, leaping into the air.

"Ooh, Miss Scarum, you've gone as white as a ghost," said Wanda Witch.

"Tee hee," laughed Bonyparte the skeleton. "He certainly scared you."

"Come here!" boomed Miss Scarum.

Little Ghost shook with fear, but Miss Scarum just laughed, went to her desk, and produced a certificate.

"I think we can say you've passed your scaring exam now," she said.

Little Ghost opened his eyes wide with surprise and then he smiled—just a ghost of a smile.

Editor
Lorin Klistoff, M.A.

Managing Editor
Karen Goldfluss, M.S. Ed.

Editor-in-Chief
Sharon Coan, M.S. Ed.

Cover Artist
Barb Lorseyedi

Art Coordinator
Kevin Barnes

Art Director
CJae Froshay

Imaging
James Edward Grace

Product Manager
Phil Garcia

Publisher
Mary D. Smith, M.S. Ed.

Practice Makes Perfect

Word Problems

GRADE 4

Includes practice for Standardized Tests

Teacher Created Resources

Author

Mary Rosenberg

Teacher Created Resources, Inc.
6421 Industry Way
Westminster, CA 92683
www.teachercreated.com

ISBN: 978-0-7439-3314-8

©2002 Teacher Created Resources, Inc.
Reprinted, 2013

Made in U.S.A.

Table of Contents

The old adage "practice makes perfect" can really hold true for your child and his or her education. The more practice and exposure your child has with concepts being taught in school, the more success he or she is likely to find. For many parents, knowing how to help their children can be frustrating because the resources may not be readily available. As a parent it is also difficult to know where to focus your efforts so that the extra practice your child receives at home supports what he or she is learning in school.

This book has been designed to help parents and teachers reinforce basic skills with their children. *Practice Makes Perfect* reviews basic math skills for children in grade 4. The math focus is word problems. While it would be impossible to include in this book all concepts taught in grade 4, the following basic objectives are reinforced through practice exercises. These objectives support math standards established on a district, state, or national level. (Refer to the Table of Contents for the specific objectives of each practice page.)

- rounding numbers
- adding and subtracting 2-digit numbers
- adding and subtracting 3-digit numbers
- adding and subtracting 4-digit numbers
- adding and subtracting 5- and 6-digit numbers
- multiplying numbers
- multiplying by 100 and 1,000

- dividing with and without remainders
- choosing operations
- working with money and time
- working with fractions
- finding the average
- estimating differences

There are 36 practice pages organized sequentially so children can build their knowledge from more basic skills to higher-level math skills. To correct the practice pages in this book, use the answer key provided on pages 47 and 48. Six practice tests follow the practice pages. These provide children with multiple-choice test items to help prepare them for standardized tests administered in schools. As children complete a problem, they fill in the correct letter among the answer choices. An optional "bubble-in" answer sheet has also been provided on page 46. This answer sheet is similar to those found on standardized tests. As your child completes each test, he or she can fill in the correct bubbles on the answer sheet.

How to Make the Most of This Book

Here are some useful ideas for optimizing the practice pages in this book:

- Set aside a specific place in your home to work on the practice pages. Keep it neat and tidy with materials on hand.
- Set up a certain time of day to work on the practice pages. This will establish consistency. An alternative is to look for times in your day or week that are less hectic and more conducive to practicing skills.
- Keep all practice sessions with your child positive and constructive. If the mood becomes tense or you and your child are frustrated, set the book aside and look for another time to practice with your child.
- Help with instructions if necessary. If your child is having difficulty understanding what to do or how to get started, work the first problem through with him or her.
- Review the work your child has done. This serves as reinforcement and provides further practice.
- Allow your child to use whatever writing instruments he or she prefers. For example, colored pencils can add variety and pleasure to drill work.
- Pay attention to the areas in which your child has the most difficulty. Provide extra guidance and exercises in those areas. Allowing children to use drawings and manipulatives, such as coins, tiles, game markers, or flash cards, can help them grasp difficult concepts more easily.
- Look for ways to make real-life application to the skills being reinforced.

Practice 1 ꙮ ꙮ ꙮ ꙮ ꙮ ꙮ ꙮ ꙮ ꙮ ꙮ ꙮ

When rounding to the nearest hundred, look at the number in the tens place. If the number is 5 or larger, round up. If the number is less than 5, round down.

Examples:	1<u>6</u>9 ➤ 200	1<u>3</u>0 ➤ 100

Read each word problem. Round the numbers to the nearest hundred. Then add or subtract.

1. Rodney had 552 Canadian coins and 279 English coins. About how many coins did he have altogether?

$$
\begin{array}{r}
5\underline{5}2 \\
+\ 2\underline{7}9 \\
\end{array}
\ \to\
\begin{array}{r}
600 \\
+\ 300 \\
\end{array}
$$

2. Olivia had 801 German coins and 80 French coins. About how many coins did she have altogether?

$$
\begin{array}{r}
801 \\
+\ 80 \\
\end{array}
\ \to\
\begin{array}{r}
\underline{} \\
+\ \underline{} \\
\end{array}
$$

3. Elliot had 106 Russian coins and 340 Austrian coins. About how many coins does he have altogether?

$$
\begin{array}{r}
106 \\
+\ 340 \\
\end{array}
\ \to\
\begin{array}{r}
\underline{} \\
+\ \underline{} \\
\end{array}
$$

4. Amy's motorcycle trip is 699 miles. She has ridden 380 miles. About how many more miles does she have to go?

$$
\begin{array}{r}
699 \\
-\ 380 \\
\end{array}
\ \to\
\begin{array}{r}
\underline{} \\
-\ \underline{} \\
\end{array}
$$

5. Matt's bicycle trip is 981 miles. He has ridden 176 miles. About how many more miles does he have to go?

$$
\begin{array}{r}
981 \\
-\ 176 \\
\end{array}
\ \to\
\begin{array}{r}
\underline{} \\
-\ \underline{} \\
\end{array}
$$

6. Erin's airplane trip is 349 miles. She has flown 153 miles. About how many more miles does she have to go?

$$
\begin{array}{r}
349 \\
-\ 153 \\
\end{array}
\ \to\
\begin{array}{r}
\underline{} \\
-\ \underline{} \\
\end{array}
$$

Practice 2

Read each word problem. Write the number sentence it shows. Find the sum.

1. In the forest, Lisa counted 83 pine trees, 24 spider webs, and 16 chipmunks. How many things did she count in all?

_____ + _____ + _____ = _____

2. In Bill's classroom there are 47 pencils, 21 pieces of chalk, and 33 bottles of glue. How many supplies are there in all?

_____ + _____ + _____ = _____

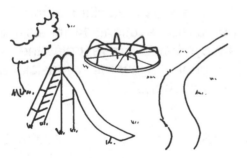

3. At the park, Carla counted 14 ducks, 32 children, and 24 roller skates. How many things did she count in all?

_____ + _____ + _____ = _____

4. James counted 36 stars one night, 42 stars the next, and 87 on the third night. How many stars did he count in all?

_____ + _____ + _____ = _____

Practice 3 ❧ ❧ ❧ ❧ ❧ ❧ ❧ ❧ ❧ ❧ ❧ ❧ ❧ ❧ ❧ ❧

Read each word problem. Decide how to solve it. Then circle *add* or *subtract*.

1. There are 95 musicians in the woodwinds section. 50 of the musicians play flutes. The rest play clarinets. How many musicians play clarinets?

   add   subtract

2. There are 37 trombones and 40 tuba players in the brass section of the orchestra. How many musicians are there in all?

   add   subtract

3. There are 35 musicians in the strings section. 13 musicians play violas. The rest play cellos. How many musicians play the cello?

   add   subtract

4. In the percussion section there are 17 bass drums and 40 side drums. How many drums are there in all?

   add   subtract

5. In the woodwinds section there are 56 oboes and 16 piccolos. How many instruments are in the woodwinds section?

   add   subtract

6. There are 59 musicians in the percussion section. 11 musicians play the cymbals. The rest play the xylophone. How many musicians play the xylophone?

   add   subtract

7. Solve the problem.

   In the High Society Symphony, there are 22 harps, 43 violas, 59 trumpets, and 92 saxophones. How many instruments are there in the High Society Symphony?

   There are _____ instruments in the High Society Symphony.

Practice 4 ๑ ๏ ๑ ๏ *Practice* ๏ ๑ ๏ ๑ ๏ ๑ ๏ ๑ ๏ ๑ ๏

Solve each problem. Show your work.

1. Old MacDonald had 379 sheep, 108 pigs, and 135 chickens. How many animals are there in all?

   There are _____ animals in all.

2. Old MacDonald had 912 bulls and 516 cows. How many more bulls than cows are there?

   There are _____ more bulls than cows.

3. Old MacDonald had 298 goats and 187 kids (baby goats). How many more goats than kids are there?

   There are _____ more goats than kids.

4. Old MacDonald's children have pets. The children have 154 cats, 152 dogs, and 315 mice. How many pets are there in all?

   There are _____ pets in all.

5. Old MacDonald had 733 bales of hay. He fed 279 of the bales of hay to the horses. How many bales of hay are left?

   There are _____ bales of hay left.

6. Old MacDonald has 108 horses in the barn, 693 horses in the pasture, and 160 horses rounding up the cows. How many horses are there in all?

   There are _____ horses in all.

7. Which animal does Old MacDonald have the most of?_____

8. Which animal does Old MacDonald have the fewest of?_____

9. Which one of Old MacDonald's animals has only 2 legs?_____

10. Are there more pets or more horses? _____

Practice 5 ⟳ ⟲ ⟳ ⟲ ⟳ ⟲ ⟳ ⟲ ⟳ ⟲ ⟳ ⟲ ⟳ ⟲

Solve each word problem. Show your work.

1. The carnival sold 1,542 adult passes; 4,791 senior passes; and 9,148 children's passes. How many passes were sold?

   The carnival sold _____ passes.

2. There were 2,067 people waiting in line for the ferris wheel. An hour later, there were still 1,841 people waiting in line. How many people had their turn on the ferris wheel?

   _____ people had their turn.

3. The popcorn man sold 5,076 tubs of popcorn. 2,291 of the tubs of popcorn did not have any butter. How many tubs of popcorn did have butter?

   _____ tubs of popcorn had butter.

4. The snack bar sold 5,027 servings of cotton candy; 2,386 bags of peanuts, and 1,081 snow cones. How many snacks did the snack bar sell?

   The snack bar sold _____ snacks.

5. The Hot Dog Hut sold 7,356 hot dogs. 5,861 of the hot dogs were on sticks. How many hot dogs were not on sticks?

   _____ hot dogs were not on sticks.

6. At the prize booth, the people were given 4,104 stuffed bears; 8,677 stuffed bunnies; and 3,437 stuffed pigs. How many prizes were given away?

   _____ prizes were given away.

Practice 6 ꩜ ꩜ ꩜ ꩜ ꩜ ꩜ ꩜ ꩜ ꩜ ꩜ ꩜ ꩜ ꩜

Solve each word problem. Show your work.

1. Hope gathered 56,329 pounds of walnuts and 10,428 pounds of pecans. How many pounds of nuts did Hope gather in all?

   Hope gathered _____ pounds of nuts in all.

2. Godfrey picked 34,159 pounds of corn and 11,724 pounds of peas. How many pounds of vegetables did Godfrey gather in all?

   Godfrey gathered _____ pounds of vegetables in all.

3. Mom earned 573,319 frequent flier miles. Dad earned 421,569 frequent flier miles. How many frequent flier miles did they earn in all?

   They earned _____ frequent flier miles in all.

4. Grandma has traveled 765,863 miles. Grandpa has traveled 134,018 miles. How many miles have they traveled in all?

   They have traveled _____ miles in all.

5. Jim Brown rushed for 12,312 yards. Franco Harris rushed 12,120 yards. How many more yards did Jim Brown rush?

   Jim Brown rushed _____ more yards.

6. A doctor earns $59,300 a year while a secretary earns $20,600 a year. How much more does a doctor earn?

   A doctor earns _____ more.

Practice 7 ⟳ ◔ ⟳ ◔ ⟳ ◔ ⟳ ◔ ⟳ ◔ ⟳ ◔ ⟳ ◔ ⟳ ◔ ⟳ ◔ ⟳

Solve each word problem. Show your work.

1. The first crossword puzzle was made in 1913. 20 years later, the first comic book was published. What was the year?

   The first comic book was published in _____.

2. The first toy balloon was made in 1825. 42 years earlier, the first hot air balloon was made. What was the year?

   The first hot air balloon was made in _____.

3. In 1767 the first jigsaw puzzle was made. 164 years later, a jigsaw puzzle game was invented. What was the year?

   The first jigsaw puzzle game was invented in _____.

4. Velcro™ was first introduced in 1948. 23 years earlier, clear tape was first made. What was the year?

   Clear tape was invented in _____.

5. In 1920 the first hair dryer was made. 150 years earlier the first toothbrush was invented. What was the year?

   The first toothbrush was invented in _____.

6. The first pair of roller skates was made in 1759. 158 years later, the first pair of tennis shoes was made. What was the year?

   The first pair of tennis shoes was made in _____.

7. Write the years for each invention in order, from earliest to most recent.

   _____, _____, _____, _____, _____, _____,

   _____, _____, _____, _____, _____, _____

Practice 8 ⟳ ⟳ ⟳ ⟳ ⟳ ⟳ ⟳ ⟳ ⟳ ⟳ ⟳ ⟳

Solve each word problem. Show your work and circle your answer.

1. Marshall delivers 37 newspapers. Logan delivers 3 times more newspapers than Marshall. Joe delivers twice as many newspapers than Logan. How many newspapers does Joe deliver?

111	151	222

2. Tina collected 36 aluminum cans. Gina collected twice as many cans as Tina. Lina collected 16 more cans than Gina. How many cans did Lina collect?

72	84	88

3. Raquel gathered 71 pinecones. Randy gathered 10 more pinecones than Raquel. Rochelle gathered 5 times as many as Randy. How many pinecones did Rochelle gather?

405	455	505

4. Nagene read 55 pages in the book. Norman read 4 times as many pages than Nagene. Nancy read 20 more pages than Norman. How many pages did Nancy read?

200	220	240

5. Albert has 26 stickers. Arnold has 8 times as many stickers as Albert. Amy has 9 fewer stickers than Arnold. How many stickers does Amy have?

219	208	199

6. Joe has 47 baseball cards. Jack has 3 times as many baseball cards as Joe. Danny has 4 fewer baseball cards than Jack. How many baseball cards does Danny have?

141	137	145

Practice 9   ᕫ ᕫ ᕫ ᕫ ᕫ ᕫ ᕫ ᕫ ᕫ ᕫ ᕫ ᕫ

Solve each word problem. Show your work and circle your answer.

1. Maggie counted 394 spiders. Each spider had 8 legs. How many legs are there in all?

   3,152 legs   3,512 legs

2. Alan counted 684 horses. Each horse had 4 legs. How many legs are there in all?

   2,736 legs   2,376 legs

3. Jeremy counted 103 starfish. Each starfish had 5 legs. How many legs are there in all?

   551 legs   515 legs

4. Carol counted 110 octopuses. Each octopus had 8 legs. How many legs are there in all?

   880 legs   808 legs

5. Heather counted 653 ants. Each ant had 6 legs. How many legs are there in all?

   3,819 legs   3,918 legs

6. Tracy counted 378 birds. Each bird had 2 legs. How many legs are there in all?

   756 legs   765 legs

7. Mel counted 918 fish. Each fish had 0 legs. How many legs are there in all?

   918 legs   0 legs

8. Jenna counted 972 flamingos. Each flamingo was standing on one leg. How many legs are standing in all?

   972 legs   1,944 legs

Practice 10 ᕉ ᕉ ᕉ ᕉ ᕉ ᕉ ᕉ ᕉ ᕉ ᕉ ᕉ ᕉ

Solve each word problem. Show your work.

1. Peter sold 10 boxes of stars. Each box contains 17 stars. How many stars did Peter sell in all?

Peter sold _____ stars in all.

2. George bought 15 boxes of star-shaped cookies. Each box had 18 cookies. How many cookies did George sell in all?

George sold _____ star-shaped cookies in all.

3. Marlee bought 25 bags of buttons. Each bag had 16 star-shaped buttons. How many star-shaped buttons did Marlee buy in all?

Marlee bought _____ star-shaped buttons in all.

4. Audra made 31 ties. On each tie she sewed 43 star patches. How many star patches did Audra sew in all?

Audra sewed _____ star patches in all.

5. Anita used 26 cookie sheets. Each cookie sheet had 38 cookies decorated with star-shaped sprinkles. How many cookies did Anita bake in all?

Anita baked _____ cookies in all.

6. There are 39 members in the troop. Each member stuck 31 star-shaped flowers on the float for the parade. How many star-shaped flowers did the troop put on the float?

The troop put _____ flowers on the float.

More Multiplying

Practice 11 ⟋ ⟋ ⟋ ⟋ ⟋ ⟋ ⟋ ⟋ ⟋ ⟋ ⟋ ⟋

Solve each word problem. Show your work.

1. It takes Mercury about 88 days to complete one revolution around the sun. It takes Venus almost 3 times longer to complete one revolution. About how many days does it take Venus to complete one revolution?

   It takes Venus about _____ days.

2. It takes Earth about 365 days to complete one revolution. The planet Jupiter takes almost 12 times longer to complete one revolution. About how many days does it take Jupiter to complete one revolution?

   It takes Jupiter about _____ days.

3. It takes Saturn about 10,759 days to complete one revolution. Pluto takes more than 9 times longer to complete one revolution. About how many days does it take Pluto to complete one revolution?

   It takes Pluto about _____ days.

4. It takes Mars about 687 days to complete one revolution. It takes Neptune 45 times longer to complete one revolution. About how many days does it take Neptune to complete one revolution?

   It takes Neptune about _____ days.

5. It takes Saturn about 10,759 days to complete one revolution. Uranus takes about 3 times longer to complete one revolution. About how many days does it take Uranus to complete one revolution?

   It takes Uranus about _____ days.

6. Which planet takes the shortest amount of time to complete one revolution?

   _____

7. Which planet takes the longest amount of time to complete one revolution?

   _____

Practice 12 ➲ ❧ ➲ ❧ ➲ ❧ ➲ ❧ ➲ ❧ ➲ ❧ ➲ ❧

Solve each word problem. Show your work.

1. One cup of alphabet soup contains 312 letters. How many letters are in 100 cups of alphabet soup?

   There are _____ letters in 100 cups of alphabet soup.

2. One bowl of oatmeal has 440 oats. How many oats are in 100 bowls of oatmeal?

   There are _____ oats in 100 bowls of oatmeal.

3. One box of straight pins has 58 pins. How many pins are in 1,000 boxes?

   There are _____ pins in 1,000 boxes.

4. One jar of sprinkles has 3,429 sprinkles. How many sprinkles are in 100 jars?

   There are _____ sprinkles in 100 jars.

5. One spoonful of sugar contains 9,981 sugar granules. How many granules of sugar are in 1,000 spoonfuls?

   There are _____ sugar granules in 1,000 spoonfuls.

6. One bean bag contains 10,738 pellets. How many pellets are in 10 bean bags?

   There are _____ pellets in 10 bean bags.

7. One serving of rice has 462 grains. How many grains of rice are in 100 servings?

   There are _____ grains of rice in 100 servings.

8. One bag of carrot seeds contains 187 seeds. How many seeds are in 1,000 bags of carrot seeds?

   There are _____ carrot seeds in 1,000 bags.

Practice 13 ⊙ ⊚ ⊚ ⊚ ⊚ ⊚ ⊚ ⊚ ⊚ ⊚ ⊚ ⊚ ⊚ ⊚

Solve each word problem. Show your work.

1. The bowling alley has 10 lanes and 50 bowlers. How many bowlers are on each lane?

   There are _____ bowlers on each lane.

2. The Up-Your-Alley Snack Bar sells donuts 6 for $1.20. How much does one donut cost?

   One donut costs _____.

3. Bowling shoes are rented at the rate of $1.00 for every 5 hours. How much does it cost to rent the shoes for one hour?

   The bowling shoes cost _____ for one hour.

4. The bowling alley suggests selecting a ball that is 1/7 of the bowler's weight. If the bowler weighs 84 pounds, how much should the bowling ball weigh?

   The bowling ball should weigh _____ pounds.

5. Gertie bowled 5 games and had a total of 515 points. What was Gertie's average score?

   Gertie's average score was _____ points.

6. Jaden and Jason bought the Bowler's Special—2 hot dogs, 2 fries, and 2 sodas for $4.06. Jaden and Jason split the bill. What was each bowler's share of the bill?

   Each bowler's share of the bill was _____.

Practice 14 ᗧ ᗧ ᗧ ᗧ ᗧ ᗧ ᗧ ᗧ ᗧ ᗧ ᗧ ᗧ ᗧ ᗧ

Solve each word problem. Show your work.

1. There are 855 people on the tour. How many 9-seat tour buses are needed?

    _____ 9-seat tour buses are needed.

2. How many pairs of $8 sunglasses can be bought with $232?

    _____ pairs of $8 sunglasses can be bought.

3. The concert tickets cost $8 each. The choir has $832. How many tickets can they buy?

    The choir can buy _____ tickets.

4. There are 6,732 Fruity O's in 3 boxes. About how many Fruity O's are in each box?

    There are _____ Fruity O's in each box.

5. A camel drinks 9 gallons of water each minute. About how many minutes will it take for the camel to drink 8,829 gallons of water?

    It will take about _____ minutes.

6. A farmer had 3,200 corn plants in his field. If each row yielded 80 plants, how many rows did the farmer have in his field?

    The farmer had _____ rows in his field.

7. Each sheared sheep produces 7 pounds of wool. How many sheep were sheared to produce 1,540 pounds of wool?

    _____ sheep were sheared.

Practice 15 ꙮ ꙮ ꙮ ꙮ ꙮ ꙮ ꙮ ꙮ ꙮ ꙮ ꙮ ꙮ

Solve each word problem. Show your work and circle your answer.

1. All 416 students are going on a field trip. A bus can hold 52 students. How many buses do the students need?

6   7   8

2. 312 students decided to order pizza for lunch. Each extra large pizza has 12 slices. How many pizzas should they order so that each student will have at least one slice?

25   26   27

3. 16 students bought an elephant-size box of popcorn. The popcorn weighs 976 ounces. How many ounces of popcorn can each student eat?

51   61   71

4. The students were able to measure the boa constrictor. The boa constrictor was 360 inches long. How many feet was that?

30 ft.   36 ft.   42 ft.

5. The total ticket cost for 400 students was $1,000. How much did each student's ticket cost?

$2.50 $3.00 $3.50

6. The gas for the bus cost $72.00. Nine parents wanted to split the gas cost evenly. How much did each parent pay?

$9.00 $8.00 $7.00

Practice 16 ᕯ ᕯ ᕯ ᕯ ᕯ ᕯ ᕯ ᕯ ᕯ ᕯ ᕯ ᕯ ᕯ ᕯ ᕯ

Solve each word problem. Show your work.

1. Cal had 100 cows and 8 pastures. He puts an equal number of cows in each pasture. How many cows are left over?

$$8 \overline{) 100}$$

There are _____ cows left.

2. Sally had 43 horses and 9 barns. She put an equal number of horses in each barn. How many horses are left over?

There are _____ horses left.

3. Harry has 75 chickens divided equally among 9 pens. How many chickens are in each pen?

There are _____ chickens in each pen.

The remainder is _____.

4. Susie has 83 ducks divided equally among 9 pens. How many ducks are in each pen?

There are _____ ducks in each pen.

The remainder is _____.

5. Andy had 74 pieces of hay. He put an equal number of hay into 3 stalls. How many pieces of hay are in each stall?

There are _____ pieces of hay in each stall.

The remainder is _____.

6. Agnes had 44 eggs. She put an equal number of eggs into 7 boxes. How many eggs are in each box?

There are _____ eggs in each box.

The remainder is _____.

Practice 17 ⸙ ⟳ ⸙ ⟳ ⸙ ⟳ ⸙ ⟳ ⸙ ⟳ ⸙ ⟳ ⸙ ⟳ ⸙ ⟳ ⸙ ⟳

Solve each word problem. Show your work.

1. There were 550 spectators sitting in 50 rows. How many spectators were in each row?

   There were _____ spectators in each row.

2. There were 610 students marching in 10 bands. How many students were in each band?

   There were _____ students in each band.

3. There were 950 people watching the 10-block parade. How many people were on each block?

   There were _____ people on each block.

4. There were 300 people who paid $10.00 each to watch the parade from the Sky Box. How much money was paid in all?

   _____ was paid in all.

5. The 14 people on the clean-up crew swept up a total of 280 pounds of confetti. How many pounds of confetti did each crew member sweep up?

   Each crew member swept up _____ pounds of confetti.

6. After the parade, all 306 students from the local school went to the park for a picnic. Each student ate 10 hot dogs. How many hot dogs did they eat in all?

   The students ate _____ hot dogs in all.

Practice 18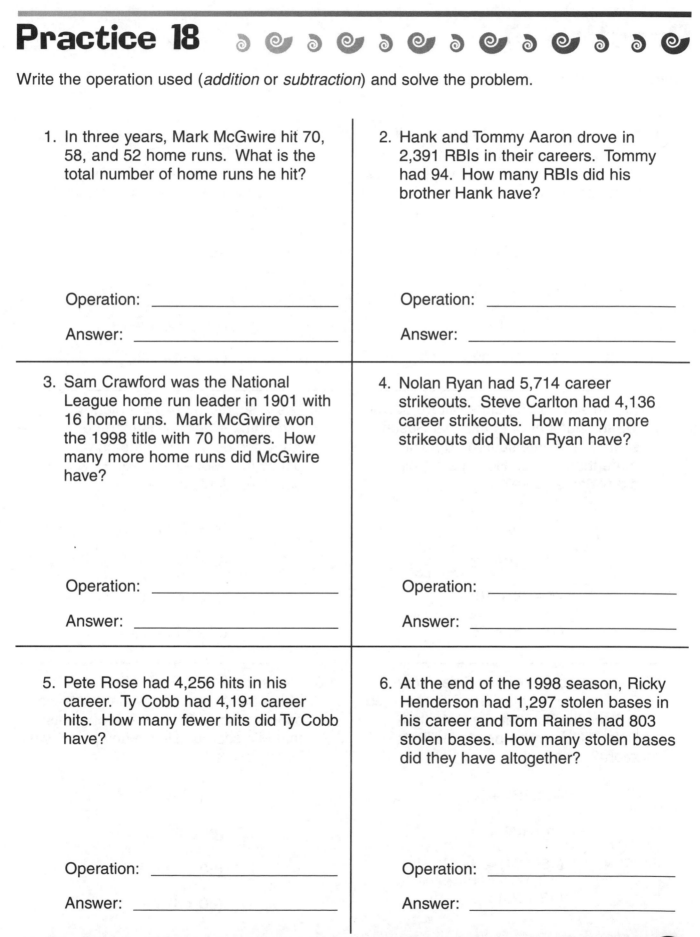

Write the operation used (*addition* or *subtraction*) and solve the problem.

1. In three years, Mark McGwire hit 70, 58, and 52 home runs. What is the total number of home runs he hit?

   Operation: _____

   Answer: _____

2. Hank and Tommy Aaron drove in 2,391 RBIs in their careers. Tommy had 94. How many RBIs did his brother Hank have?

   Operation: _____

   Answer: _____

3. Sam Crawford was the National League home run leader in 1901 with 16 home runs. Mark McGwire won the 1998 title with 70 homers. How many more home runs did McGwire have?

   Operation: _____

   Answer: _____

4. Nolan Ryan had 5,714 career strikeouts. Steve Carlton had 4,136 career strikeouts. How many more strikeouts did Nolan Ryan have?

   Operation: _____

   Answer: _____

5. Pete Rose had 4,256 hits in his career. Ty Cobb had 4,191 career hits. How many fewer hits did Ty Cobb have?

   Operation: _____

   Answer: _____

6. At the end of the 1998 season, Ricky Henderson had 1,297 stolen bases in his career and Tom Raines had 803 stolen bases. How many stolen bases did they have altogether?

   Operation: _____

   Answer: _____

Carissa

Choosing Operations

Practice 19 ⟳ ⟳ ⟳ ⟳ ⟳ ⟳ ⟳ ⟳ ⟳ ⟳ ⟳ ⟳

Read each word problem. Circle the correct operation.

1. Dot scored 93 points. Rob scored twice as many points as Dot. Herman scored 32 fewer points than Rob. How many points did Herman score?

93 – (32 x 2)

93 x (32 – 2)

(93 – 32) x 2

(93 x 2) – 32

2. Becky scored 19 points. Sean scored 46 more points than Becky. Jed scored twice the number of points than Sean did. How many points did Jed score?

(46 x 19) + 19

19 + (46 x 2)

(19 + 46) x 2

(19 x 46) x 2

3. Susan scored 75 points. Steve scored 1/3 the number of points that Susan scored. Melanie scored 10 points more than Steve. How many points did Melanie score?

(75 ÷ 3) + 10

(75 ÷ 10) + 3

75 ÷ (3 + 10)

(10 ÷ 3) + 75

4. Leslie scored 65 points. Morley scored 57 fewer points than Leslie. Andy scored 10 times the number of points that Morley scored. How many points did Andy score?

(65 – 57) x 10

(65 x 10) – 57

65 – (57 x 10)

(65 x 57) – 10

5. Ben scored 45 points. Dylan scored 24 more points than Ben. Terri scored 3 times the number of points than Dylan. How many points did Terri score?

45 x (24 + 3)

45 + (24 x 3)

(45 x 24) + 3

(45 + 24) x 3

6. Lisa scored 80 points. Mia scored 1/4 of the points that Lisa scored. Noelle scored 7 times the number of points that Mia scored. How many points did Noelle score?

(80 ÷ 4) x 7

80 x (7 ÷ 4)

(80 ÷ 7) x 4

(80 x 4) ÷ 7

Practice 20 ꙮ ꙮ ꙮ ꙮ ꙮ ꙮ ꙮ ꙮ ꙮ ꙮ ꙮ ꙮ ꙮ

Estimate the differences by rounding each number to the nearest hundred and then subtracting. Circle your answer.

1. There are 323 jumbo jets and 187 puddle jumpers. What is the difference?

about 100

about 200

about 300

2. There are 258 first-class tickets and 814 coach tickets. What is the difference?

about 300

about 400

about 500

3. There are 312 chicken dinners and 439 fish dinners. What is the difference?

about 0

about 100

about 200

4. There are 110 business people and 942 families on the plane. What is the difference?

about 800

about 900

about 1,000

5. There are 976 passengers and 626 window seats. What is the difference?

about 300

about 400

about 500

6. 251 planes departed late and 662 planes departed on time. What is the difference?

about 200

about 300

about 400

Telling Time Differences

Practice 21 ⟳ ⟳ ⟳ ⟳ ⟳ ⟳ ⟳ ⟳ ⟳ ⟳ ⟳

Solve each word problem.

1. Dale leaves for school at 9:10 A.M. He arrives at school at 9:18 A.M. How many minutes does it take Dale to walk to school?

_____ minutes

2. Regina put the cookies in the oven at 9:20 A.M. She took the cookies out at 9:37 A.M. How many minutes did the cookies bake?

_____ minutes

3. Edna began playing the piano at 10:10 A.M. and finished at 10:45 A.M. How long did Edna practice?

_____ minutes

4. Garrett started cleaning the tub at 2:44 P.M. and finished at 2:59 P.M. How long did it take Garrett to clean the tub?

_____ minutes

5. Tobias left the library at 2:10 P.M. and arrived back home at 2:55 P.M. How long did it take Tobias to walk home?

_____ minutes

6. Ruby left for the mall at 6:41 P.M. and reached the mall at 6:47 P.M. How long did it take Ruby to walk to the mall?

_____ minutes

Practice 22 ⟨spiral decorations⟩

Solve each word problem. Rewrite the time in hours and minutes.

1. Annette practices the piano every day for 20 minutes. How many minutes does Annette practice in one week?

   _____ minutes or

   _____ hours _____ minutes

2. Starla goes to gymnastics class 3 times a week for 45 minutes each time. How many minutes does Starla spend in gymnastics class in one week?

   _____ minutes or

   _____ hours _____ minutes

3. Nick has baseball practice 4 times a week. Each practice lasts 90 minutes. How many minutes each week does Nick have baseball practice?

   _____ minutes or

   _____ hours _____ minutes

4. Elisabeth sings twice a week for 50 minutes each time. How many minutes each week does Elisabeth sing?

   _____ minutes or

   _____ hours _____ minutes

5. Max jogs 4 times a week for 35 minutes each time. How many minutes does Max jog each week?

   _____ minutes or

   _____ hours _____ minutes

6. Harry lifts weights 4 times each week. He spends 30 minutes each time. How many minutes does Harry lift weights each week?

   _____ minutes or

   _____ hours _____ minutes

Practice 23 ꙍ ꙍ ꙍ ꙍ ꙍ ꙍ ꙍ ꙍ ꙍ ꙍ ꙍ ꙍ ꙍ

Write the missing departure time, flying time, or arrival time.

Departs From	Departure Time	Flying Time	Arrival Time	Arrives At
1. City A	8:03	_____ min.	8:10	City B
2. City B	_____	12 min.	8:28	City C
3. City C	_____	11 min.	8:44	City D
4. City D	9:00	7 min.	_____	City E
5. City E	9:30	25 min.	_____	City A

Solve each problem using the time schedule above. Fill in the correct answer circle.

6. How many minutes are there between arriving at City C and departing from City C?

    5 minutes   11 minutes
      ◯   ◯

7. Which takes longer, to fly from City A to City B or from City E to City A?

    City A to City B   City E to City A
      ◯   ◯

8. If you need to check in at the airport 15 minutes before the departure time, what time should you be there to fly out of City D?

    8:30   8:45
      ◯   ◯

9. If the flight from City E is delayed by 18 minutes, what time will it actually depart?

    9:12   9:48
      ◯   ◯

Practice 24 ⟳ ⟳ ⟳ ⟳ ⟳ ⟳ ⟳ ⟳ ⟳ ⟳ ⟳ ⟳ ⟳ ⟳

Write down what piece of information is needed to solve the problem.

Example: Benito went to the bakery and bought 6 cupcakes and some cookies. How many cookies did Benito buy?

Missing Information: How many items did Benito purchase in all?

(number of items in all – cupcakes = number of cookies)

---

1. Makayla has $10.00. Does she have enough to buy a soccer ball and a pair of shin guards?

    Missing Information: _____

    _____

2. Minnie's class is going on a field trip. Each bus can take 20 kids. How many buses does Minnie's class need?

    Missing Information: _____

    _____

3. Garth picked the same number of grapes as the combined total of plums and peaches he picked. How many grapes did Garth pick?

    Missing Information: _____

    _____

4. Jennifer bought a bag of jelly beans. There were 23 red jelly beans and 15 orange jelly beans. The rest were black jelly beans. How many black jelly beans were in the bag?

    Missing Information: _____

    _____

5. Cerise needs to put 10 seeds in each pot. How many seeds does Cerise need?

    Missing Information: _____

    _____

6. Oliver earned 10 more points on the spelling test than Guy. What was Oliver's score?

    Missing Information: _____

    _____

Practice 25 ෙ ෙ ෙ ෙ ෙ ෙ ෙ ෙ ෙ ෙ ෙ

Read and solve each word problem.

Money Problem #1

The Sylvester triplets broke into their piggy bank. The triplets sorted the coins into different groups. The triplets had 72 quarters, 36 dimes, 24 nickels, and 15 pennies.

1. How much money did the triplets have?

_____

2. The triplets split the money 3 ways. How much money did each triplet receive?

_____

3. Was there any money left over? (If yes, how much?)

_____

Money Problem #2

Dolph went through all of his family's jacket pockets. Dolph found 48 nickels and 73 pennies.

1. How much money did Dolph find?

_____

2. Dolph split the money into 4 cups. How much money did Dolph put in each cup?

_____

3. Was there any money left over? (If yes, how much?)

_____

Money Problem #3

Asa looked in his wallet. He found 1 ten-dollar bill, 7 five-dollar bills, and 1 one-dollar bill.

1. How much money did Asa have in his wallet?

_____

2. Asa decided to give his money to his two brothers and his two sisters. How much money did each of the children receive?

_____

3. Was there any money left over? (If yes, how much?)

_____

Money Problem #4

Ana looked in her wallet. She found 5 ten-dollar bills, 2 five-dollar bills, and 6 one-dollar bills.

1. How much money did Ana have in her wallet?

_____

2. Ana decided to give half of the money to charity and keep the rest. How much money did Ana give to charity?

_____

3. Was there any money left over? (If yes, how much?)

_____

Practice 26 ౭ ම ౭ ම ౭ ම ౭ ම ౭ ම ౭ ම ౭ ම

Solve each problem using multiplication or division. Show your work.

1. If one football costs $21.45, how much would 9 footballs cost?

Nine footballs would cost _____.

2. To keep their children active, a group of 7 parents rented a giant jumping balloon for $84.63. They split the cost evenly. How much did each parent pay?

Each parent paid _____ .

3. A bag of marbles cost $2.79 at the Toys-4-Me store. How much would it cost for 30 bags?

Thirty bags would cost _____.

4. A boys' basketball team with 5 players bought a hoop and rim for $59.95 and split the cost evenly. How much did each player pay?

Each player paid _____.

5. A bag of marbles cost $2.79. A group of 5 teachers bought 20 bags of marbles and split the cost evenly. How much did each teacher pay?

Each teacher paid _____.

6. A checkerboard game costs $12.50 at the Toys-4-Me store. How much would it cost to buy 20 checkerboard games?

20 checkerboard games would cost _____.

7. Two sisters bought a beach cruiser bike for $198.56. They split the cost evenly. How much did each sister pay?

Each sister paid _____.

Practice 27

Three girls bought a chocolate cream pie. Joanna ate $\frac{1}{4}$ of the pie. Michelle ate $\frac{3}{8}$ of the pie. How much was left for Sara?

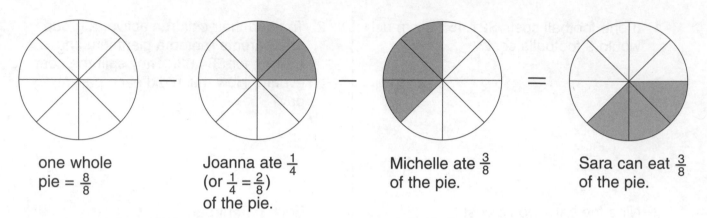

| one whole pie = $\frac{8}{8}$ | Joanna ate $\frac{1}{4}$ (or $\frac{1}{4} = \frac{2}{8}$) of the pie. | Michelle ate $\frac{3}{8}$ of the pie. | Sara can eat $\frac{3}{8}$ of the pie. |

Solve these fraction word problems.

1. Susan and Julie bought a ham and pineapple pizza. Susan ate $\frac{3}{7}$ of the pizza. How much was left for Julie? _____

2. Your best friend and you go to Pie Palace for pie. You eat $\frac{5}{6}$ of the pie. How much pie is left for your friend? _____

3. Your baseball coach bought a pizza to share with the team. The coach ate $\frac{7}{10}$ of the pizza. How much pizza was left for the team? _____

4. Your dad bought one whole vegetarian pizza from Pizza Palace. Your sister ate $\frac{5}{8}$ of the pizza before you got home. How much pizza was left for you? _____

5. James and Ralph bought a jalepeno pizza. James ate $\frac{2}{3}$ of the pizza. How much pizza was left for Ralph? _____

6. The third-grade teacher and the fourth-grade teacher bought a pepperoni pizza. The fourth-grade teacher ate $\frac{7}{12}$ of the pizza. How much pizza was left for the third-grade teacher? _____

7. The volleyball coach bought a sausage and olive pizza. He ate $\frac{3}{5}$ of the pizza. How much was left for his wife? _____

8. Your teacher and a friend bought a cheese pizza from Pizza Palace. Your teacher ate $\frac{1}{2}$ of the pizza. How much was left for the friend? _____

Practice 28 ⟡ ⟡ ⟡ ⟡ ⟡ ⟡ ⟡ ⟡ ⟡ ⟡ ⟡ ⟡ ⟡ ⟡

Solve each word problem. Circle your answer.

1. Edgar bought 18 apples. $\frac{1}{6}$ of them were rotten. How many apples were rotten?

3	6	9

2. Virginia bought 10 boxes of grapes. In $\frac{1}{2}$ of the boxes of grapes, the grapes had become raisins! How many of the boxes still had grapes?

4	5	6

3. Jasmine bought 9 bananas. She ate $\frac{1}{3}$ of them. How many bananas are left?

9	3	6

4. Zach won $100. He shared $\frac{1}{5}$ of the money with his friend Bud.
How much money did he give to Bud?

$20.00	$0.20	$2.00

5. Mickey's Used Car Lot had 15 cars. Mickey sold $\frac{1}{3}$ of the cars over the weekend. How many of the cars did Mickey sell?

3	5	7

6. Laverne's dog had 8 puppies. Laverne gave $\frac{3}{4}$ of the puppies away. How many puppies did Laverne give away?

2	4	6

Practice 29 ⟳ ⟲ ⟳ ⟲ ⟳ ⟲ ⟳ ⟲ ⟳ ⟲ ⟳ ⟲ ⟳

Add the fractions. Show your work. Reduce to the simplest form.

1. To make granola, mix together $\frac{3}{8}$ of a cup of cereal with $\frac{1}{6}$ of a cup of honey. How many cups of granola will the recipe make?

$$\frac{3}{8} + \frac{1}{6} = ?$$
$$\frac{3}{8}\left(\frac{6}{6}\right) + \frac{1}{6}\left(\frac{8}{8}\right) = ?$$
$$\frac{18}{48} + \frac{8}{48} = \frac{26}{48} = \underline{\quad}$$

The recipe will make _____ of a cup of granola.

2. To make a great party mix, stir together $\frac{3}{7}$ of a cup of pretzels with $\frac{1}{4}$ of a cup of nuts. How many cups of party mix will the recipe make?

The recipe will make _____ of a cup of party mix.

3. To make fruit salad, stir together $\frac{1}{5}$ of a cup of sliced apples with $\frac{1}{6}$ of a cup of sliced pears. How many cups of fruit salad will the recipe make?

The recipe will make _____ of a cup of fruit salad.

4. To make a glass of strawberry milk, stir together $\frac{1}{7}$ of a cup of strawberry powder with $\frac{2}{5}$ of a cup of milk. How many cups of strawberry milk will the recipe make?

The recipe will make _____ of a cup of strawberry milk.

5. To make cinnamon apples, stir together $\frac{1}{2}$ of a cup of chopped apples with $\frac{2}{7}$ of a cup of cinnamon. How many cups of cinnamon apples will the recipe make?

The recipe will make _____ of a cup of cinnamon apples.

6. To make a tasty peanut butter treat, stir together $\frac{3}{4}$ of a cup of unmelted chocolate with $\frac{1}{7}$ of a cup of smooth peanut butter. How many cups will the peanut butter recipe make?

The peanut butter treat will make _____ of a cup.

Practice 30

Solve each word problem. Show your work.

---

1. The library has 40 science fiction books. This week $\frac{5}{8}$ of the books have been checked out. How many science fiction books were checked out?

    $$\frac{40}{1} \times \frac{5}{8} = \underline{\hspace{1cm}}$$

    _____ science fiction books were checked out.

2. Miss Witherspoon had 42 mystery books to place on the shelves. She placed $\frac{6}{7}$ of them on the bookshelves. How many books were left?

    $$\frac{42}{1} \times \frac{6}{7} = \underline{\hspace{1cm}}$$

    Miss Witherspoon had _____ books left to put on the shelves.

---

3. Mr. Delmonico looked in the card catalog and found 30 books on baseball. $\frac{5}{6}$ of the books had been checked out. How many books had been checked out?

    _____ books had been checked out.

4. Humphrey found 15 cookbooks. $\frac{3}{5}$ of the books had been written by his favorite chef, Paloma Pizza. How many of the books did the chef write?

    Paloma Pizza wrote _____ cookbooks.

---

5. Giselle loves joke books. The library has 16 joke books. Giselle has read $\frac{1}{8}$ of them. How many joke books has Giselle read?

    Giselle has read _____ joke books.

6. Billy loves looking at picture books. The library has 25. $\frac{1}{5}$ of the picture books have words as well as pictures. How many books have words and pictures?

    _____ books have words and pictures.

Practice 31 ෬ ෨ ෬ ෨ ෬ ෨ ෬ ෨ ෬ ෨ ෬ ෨ ෬ ෨ ෬ ෨ ෬

Read and solve each word problem. Show your work. Rewrite the answer as a mixed fraction.

1. Alexander mixed together $\frac{1}{2}$ of a cup of melted carmel with $\frac{2}{3}$ of a cup of popcorn. How many cups will the mixture make?

$$\frac{1}{2} + \frac{2}{3} = ?$$
$$\frac{1}{2}\left(\frac{3}{3}\right) + \frac{2}{3}\left(\frac{2}{2}\right) = ?$$
$$\frac{3}{6} + \frac{4}{6} = \frac{7}{6} = ?$$

The mixture will make _____ cups of mix.

2. Sigmund made a sandwich. He put $\frac{1}{3}$ of a cup of peanut butter and $\frac{5}{7}$ of a cup of jelly on the bread. How much peanut butter and jelly did Sigmund use?

Sigmund used _____ cups of peanut butter and jelly.

3. Gunther made a tasty punch. He mixed together $\frac{5}{6}$ of a cup of soda with $\frac{7}{8}$ of a cup of punch. How much punch did Gunther make?

Gunther made _____ cups of punch.

4. Adele made banana pancake batter. She mixed together $\frac{3}{8}$ of a cup of mashed bananas with $\frac{3}{4}$ of a cup of pancake mix. How much batter did Adele make?

Adele made _____ cups of pancake batter.

5. Demetria mixed $\frac{5}{8}$ of a cup of detergent and $\frac{4}{5}$ of a cup of cold water to use as a stain remover. How much stain remover did Demetria make?

Demetria made _____ cups of stain remover.

6. Douglas made his favorite juice. He mixed together $\frac{3}{4}$ of a cup of orange juice with $\frac{2}{5}$ of a cup of pomegranate juice. How much juice did Douglas make?

Douglas made _____ cups of juice.

Practice 32 ❧ ❧ ❧ ❧ ❧ ❧ ❧ ❧ ❧ ❧ ❧ ❧ ❧ ❧

Solve each word problem. Show your work.

1. Hercules has $\frac{3}{5}$ of a cup of sugar. The recipe calls for $\frac{1}{4}$ of a cup of sugar. How much sugar will Hercules have left?

$$\frac{3}{5} - \frac{1}{4} = ?$$
$$\frac{3}{5}\left(\frac{4}{4}\right) - \frac{1}{4}\left(\frac{5}{5}\right) = ?$$
$$\frac{12}{20} - \frac{5}{20} = \underline{\quad}$$

Hercules will have _____ of a cup of sugar left.

2. Henrietta has $\frac{1}{2}$ cup of water. She uses $\frac{2}{7}$ of the water to water her plant. How much water does Henrietta have left?

Henrietta has _____ of a cup of water left.

3. Aurora has $\frac{6}{7}$ of a cup of milk. She uses $\frac{1}{5}$ of a cup of milk to make pancake batter. How much milk does Aurora have left?

Aurora has _____ of a cup of milk left.

4. Keenan has $\frac{3}{4}$ of a quart of motor oil. He puts $\frac{1}{8}$ of a quart of oil in his car. How much oil does Keenan have left?

Keenan has _____ of a quart of motor oil left.

5. Ulysses has $\frac{2}{3}$ of a cup of butter. He puts $\frac{2}{7}$ of a cup of butter on his toast. How much butter is left?

There is _____ of a cup of butter left.

6. Jennifer had $\frac{4}{7}$ of a cup of bread crumbs. She used $\frac{2}{5}$ of a cup of bread crumbs making a recipe. How much bread crumbs does Jennifer have left?

Jennifer has _____ of a cup of bread crumbs left.

Practice 33 ⊘ ☙ ⊘ ☙ ⊘ ☙ ⊘ ☙ ⊘ ☙ ⊘ ☙ ⊘ ☙ ⊘ ☙ ⊘ ☙ ⊘

Use the above formulas to solve each word problem. Fill in the correct answer circle.

Temperature: °C → °F ___ ° C x 9 ÷ 5 + 32 = _____ ° F Example: 5° C = 41° F	**Measurement:** cm → in. _____ cm x .39 = _____ in. Example: 10 cm = 3.9 in.
Liquid: L → gal. ___ L x .26 = _____ gal. Example: 2 L = .52 gal.	**Weight:** kg → lb. _____ kg x 2.2 = _____ lb. Example: 4 kg = 8.8 lb.

1. The kids can go swimming if the outdoor temperature is 90° F. The thermostat registers 20° C. Can the kids go swimming?

   Yes   No
   ◯   ◯

2. To go on the roller coaster, a person needs to be 36 inches tall. Jason was 32 inches tall last year. He grew 5 cm during the year. Is he tall enough to go on the roller coaster?

   Yes   No
   ◯   ◯

3. The pitcher holds 1 gallon of water. Shirley needs 2 liters of water. Is the pitcher large enough to hold that much water?

   Yes   No
   ◯   ◯

4. Fido weighs 8 pounds. Sparky weighs 12 kg. Which dog weighs more?

   Fido   Sparky
   ◯   ◯

5. Central High's standing long jump record is 35 inches. Pam jumped 100 cm. Did Pam break the record?

   Yes   No
   ◯   ◯

Practice 34 ੭ ੭ ੭ ੭ ੭ ੭ ੭ ੭ ੭ ੭ ੭ ੭ ੭ ੭

Solve each problem by adding the totals and then dividing. The first one has been started for you.

1. John knocked down 7 bowling pins the first time, 8 pins the second time, and 9 pins the third time. What is John's average score?

$$\frac{7 + 8 + 9}{3} =$$

John's average score is _____.

2. Angela knocked down 10 pins the first time, 5 the second time, and 6 pins the third time. What is Angela's average score?

Angela's average score is _____.

3. Warren's bowling scores were 176, 194, and 149. What is Warren's bowling average?

Warren's bowling average is _____.

4. Grace's bowling scores were 143, 138, and 112. What is Grace's bowling average?

Grace's bowling average is _____.

5. Each night a different number of people attended the bowling tournament: 653, 375, 491, and 705. What is the average number of people that attended the tournament?

The average number is _____.

6. The Bowling Beauties' team scores were 199, 200, 305, and 280. What was their average score?

Their average score was _____.

Practice 35 ৩ ৩ ৩ ৩ ৩ ৩ ৩ ৩ ৩ ৩ ৩ ৩ ৩ ৩

Calculate the average for each of the problems. The first one has been started for you.

1. Shawna had 3 math grades: 80, 90, and 100. What was her average math grade?

$$\frac{80 + 90 + 100}{3} =$$

Her average math grade was _____.

2. James had 3 science grades: 60, 70, and 80. What was his average science grade?

His average science grade was _____.

3. Susan had 4 social studies grades: 93, 86, 70, and 71. What was her average social studies grade?

Her average social studies grade was _____.

4. The weights of 5 puppies were: 12 pounds, 39 pounds, 15 pounds, 24 pounds, and 30 pounds. What was their average weight?

Their average weight was _____ pounds.

5. The weights of 5 rocks were: 12 pounds, 48 pounds, 18 pounds, 32 pounds, and 35 pounds. What was the average weight?

The average weight was _____ pounds.

6. In the zoo, the weights of 6 bears were: 57 pounds, 130 pounds, 99 pounds, 97 pounds, 88 pounds, and 63 pounds. What was their average weight?

Their average weight was _____ pounds.

Practice 36 ⟳ ⟳ ⟳ ⟳ ⟳ ⟳ ⟳ ⟳ ⟳ ⟳ ⟳ ⟳ ⟳ ⟳ ⟳

Make a chart to help you solve these problems.

1. Loren is taller than Mike but not as tall as Sue. Ray is taller than Sue. Who is the tallest?

short ⟵————|————|————|————|————⟶ tall
        Mike Loren Sue Ray

_____ is the tallest.

2. Tim jumped farther than Darren but not as far as Loren. Maggie jumped farther than Loren but not as far as Nicky. Who jumped the farthest? Who jumped the shortest?

_____ jumped the farthest.

_____ jumped the shortest.

3. Nicky is stronger than Roy but not as strong as Loren. Darren is not as strong as Roy. Who is the strongest? Who is the weakest?

_____ is the strongest.

_____ is the weakest.

4. Darren slept longer than Ty but not as long as Sue. Loren slept longer than Sue but not as long as Roy. Who slept the longest? Who had the least sleep?

_____ slept the longest.

_____ had the least sleep.

5. Sue ate more than Loren but not as much as Nicky. Darren ate less than Loren. Who ate the most? Who ate the least?

_____ ate the most.

_____ ate the least.

6. Larry is shorter than Loren but taller than Sue. Darren is shorter than Sue but taller than Nicky. Roy is taller than Loren. Who is the shortest?

_____ is the shortest.

Test Practice 1 ⟳ ⟲ ⟳ ⟲ ⟳ ⟲ ⟳ ⟲ ⟳ ⟲ ⟳ ⟳ ⟲

Solve each problem and fill in the correct answer circle.

1. Round each number to the nearest hundred and then solve.

   Brianne painted 414 ladybugs, 163 butterflies, and 229 caterpillars on the garden mural. How many bugs did Brianne paint in all?

   (A) 800   (B) 700
   (C) 900   (D) 600

2. Round each amount to the nearest dollar and then solve.

   Jasper had $10.17. He spent $4.55 buying a new paintbrush. How much money does Jasper have left?

   (A) $16.00   (B) $15.00
   (C) $6.00   (D) $5.00

3. Round each number to the nearest hundred and then solve.

   855 people signed up for the etymology class. On the first day of class only 723 people were in attendance. How many people did not show up on the first day of class?

   (A) 200   (B) 100
   (C) 300   (D) 400

4. Solve.

   Graham is making a coconut cake. He mixed together $\frac{1}{3}$ of a cup of coconut with $\frac{1}{2}$ of a cup of butter. How many cups of ingredients did Graham use?

   (A) $\frac{6}{5}$ (B) $\frac{5}{6}$
   (C) $\frac{2}{5}$ (D) $\frac{1}{5}$

5. Solve.

   Inez gathered 18 eggs. She used $\frac{1}{3}$ of the eggs to make pancakes for breakfast. How many eggs did Inez use?

   (A) 6   (B) 12
   (C) 3   (D) 16

6. Solve.

   Andy had 44 candy bars. He put an equal number of candy bars into 7 boxes. How many candy bars are left over?

   (A) 1 candy bar   (B) 2 candy bars
   (C) 3 candy bars   (D) 4 candy bars

#3314 Practice Makes Perfect: Word Problems (Grade 4)   © Teacher Created Resources, Inc.

Test Practice 2 ෨ ෧ ෨ ෧ ෨ ෧ ෨ ෧ ෨ ෧ ෨ ෧

Solve each problem and fill in the correct answer circle.

1. Orville Wright was born in 1871. Thirty-two years later, Orville flew the first powered airplane for 12 seconds. What was the year?

Ⓐ 1903 Ⓑ 1900
Ⓒ 1904 Ⓓ 1902

2. Choose the appropriate operation.

In three baseball seasons, Jason hit 20, 27, and 16 home runs. What is the total?

Ⓐ addition Ⓑ subtraction
Ⓒ multiplying Ⓓ division

3. The Granite Stadium can hold 18,435 fans. At today's soccer game there are 6,911 empty seats. How many fans are at the soccer game?

Ⓐ 11,524 Ⓑ 25,346
Ⓒ 11,425 Ⓓ 6,911

4. The Hot Air Balloon Society has 31,978 people who fly hot air balloons and 23,875 people who chase the hot air balloons. How many members belong to The Hot Air Balloon Society?

Ⓐ 55,853 Ⓑ 55,358
Ⓒ 8,103 Ⓓ 31,978

5. The directions said to bake the brownies for a quarter to half an hour. How many minutes is that?

Ⓐ 5–20 min. Ⓑ 10–25 min.
Ⓒ 15–30 min. Ⓓ 30–45 min.

6. Trudy has to be home in $\frac{1}{6}$ of an hour. How many minutes is that?

Ⓐ 6 min. Ⓑ 8 min.
Ⓒ 10 min. Ⓓ 15 min.

Test Practice 3 ꙮ ꙮ ꙮ ꙮ ꙮ ꙮ ꙮ ꙮ ꙮ ꙮ ꙮ ꙮ

Solve each problem and fill in the correct answer circle.

1. Sid practices the violin every day for 8 minutes. He finished practicing at 10:45. What time did Sid begin practicing?

   Ⓐ 10:36　　　Ⓑ 10:37　　　Ⓒ 10:53　　　Ⓓ 10:35

2. The Day Hikers Club hiked 5 miles. How many kilometers did they hike?
   (Hint: 1 mile = 1.6 km)

   Ⓐ 5 km　　　Ⓑ 6 km　　　Ⓒ 7 km　　　Ⓓ 8 km

Train Schedule

Departs from		Arrives at	
Downtown	1:13	Midtown	1:35
Midtown	1:42	Uptown	1:59
Uptown	2:06	Downtown	2:19

Use the above schedule to answer questions 3–5.

3. How many minutes does it take to go from Downtown to Midtown?

   Ⓐ 22 minutes　　　Ⓑ 46 minutes　　　Ⓒ 29 minutes　　　Ⓓ 37 minutes

4. How many minutes does the train wait after arriving at Uptown and before leaving to another town?

   Ⓐ 7 minutes　　　Ⓑ 6 minutes　　　Ⓒ 5 minutes　　　Ⓓ 17 minutes

5. How many minutes does it take the train to go from Midtown and arrive at Uptown?

   Ⓐ 17 minutes　　　Ⓑ 18 minutes　　　Ⓒ 24 minutes　　　Ⓓ 20 minutes

6. Find the missing piece of information.

   At last week's football game, the Bears beat the Panthers. The Panthers only scored 6 points. How many points did the Bears score?

   Ⓐ the date of the game　　　　　　Ⓑ the color of the Bears' uniform
   Ⓒ how many points the Bear won by　Ⓓ the number of penalties the Bears had

Test Practice 4 ⟩ ⟳ ⟳ ⟳ ⟳ ⟳ ⟳ ⟳ ⟳ ⟳ ⟳ ⟳ ⟳ ⟳

Solve each problem and fill in the correct answer circle.

1. The PeeWee Baseball Players have a total of 120 players on 10 different teams. How many players are on each team?

   Ⓐ 10   Ⓑ 12
   Ⓒ 18   Ⓓ 20

2. Each one of the 15 students brought 10 cans of food for the canned food drive. How many cans of food are there in all?

   Ⓐ 15   Ⓑ 100
   Ⓒ 150   Ⓓ 1,500

3. Each one of the 36 Chess Club members raised $10.00 selling chocolate chess pieces. How much money did the Chess Club raise?

   Ⓐ $3.60   Ⓑ $36.00
   Ⓒ $360.00   Ⓓ $3,600.00

4. The Big Band of Riverbend raised $1,832 to buy eight new band uniforms. How much does one uniform cost?

   Ⓐ $22.90   Ⓑ $229.00
   Ⓒ $292.00   Ⓓ $299.00

5. Choose the correct math sentence.

Brad had 8 pencils. Rachel had 10 pencils. Jackie had $\frac{1}{2}$ the number of pencils that Brad and Rachel had. How many pencils does Jackie have?

   Ⓐ (8 x 10) ÷ 2   Ⓑ 10 + (8 ÷ 2)
   Ⓒ (10 ÷ 2) x 8   Ⓓ (8 + 10) ÷ 2

6. Roscoe collected 9 shells. Daisy collected 4 times the number of shells that Roscoe collected. Roger collected $\frac{1}{2}$ the number of shells that Daisy did. How many shells did Roger collect?

   Ⓐ 36   Ⓑ 24
   Ⓒ 18   Ⓓ 13

Test Practice 5 ᵔᵔᵔᵔᵔᵔᵔᵔᵔᵔᵔᵔᵔᵔ

Solve each problem and fill in the correct answer circle.

1. The ladybug has 6 legs. How many legs are on 88 ladybugs?

  Ⓐ 528　　Ⓑ 94
  Ⓒ 256　　Ⓓ 258

2. A pentagon has 5 sides. How many total sides are on 102 pentagons?

  Ⓐ 500　　Ⓑ 501
  Ⓒ 510　　Ⓓ 105

3. Dorian goes to a special math class 4 times a week. Each math class lasts 25 minutes. How many minutes in one week does Dorian spend at math class?

  Ⓐ 75 min.　　Ⓑ 100 min.
  Ⓒ 125 min.　　Ⓓ 105 min.

4. It is about 214 miles to fly from Paris to London. It is about 26 times farther to fly from Paris to Los Angeles. About how many miles is it from Paris to Los Angeles?

  Ⓐ 5,564　　Ⓑ 5,654
  Ⓒ 5,465　　Ⓓ 4,654

5. Kate found 8 quarters, 66 dimes, 17 nickels, and 8 pennies in her coin purse. How much money did Kate find?

  Ⓐ $9.35　　Ⓑ $9.45
  Ⓒ $8.85　　Ⓓ $9.53

6. There are 56 cards in the Super Trading Deck of Cards. Barry has collected $\frac{1}{4}$ of the cards. How many cards has Barry collected?

  Ⓐ 12　　Ⓑ 14
  Ⓒ 13　　Ⓓ 15

Test Practice 6 ꙮ ꙮ ꙮ ꙮ ꙮ ꙮ ꙮ ꙮ ꙮ ꙮ ꙮ

Solve each problem and fill in the correct answer circle.

1. Jonah mixed together $\frac{2}{3}$ of a cup of hot chocolate with $\frac{3}{5}$ of a cup of jumbo-size marshmallows. How many cups of ingredients did Jonah use?

   (A) $\frac{5}{8}$ (B) $\frac{6}{15}$ (C) $1\frac{4}{15}$ (D) $1\frac{3}{5}$

2. Jana mixed together $\frac{1}{7}$ of a cup of water with $\frac{2}{5}$ of a cup of sand. How many cups of the mixture did Jana make?

   (A) $\frac{19}{15}$ (B) $\frac{3}{12}$ (C) $\frac{35}{19}$ (D) $\frac{19}{35}$

3. Brett had $\frac{3}{4}$ of a cup of applesauce. He used $\frac{2}{3}$ of the cup to make applesauce cookies. How much applesauce does Brett have left?

   (A) $\frac{1}{12}$ (B) $\frac{12}{1}$ (C) $\frac{5}{7}$ (D) $\frac{5}{12}$

4. Each train car can hold 16 people. If 352 people bought train tickets, how many train cars will they need?

   (A) 22   (B) 23   (C) 24   (D) 25

Candy Grams Sold

Trisha	6	Ruby	3	Sinclair	3	Nicki	3
Burt	5	Tad	5	Tabitha	3		

Use the chart above to solve problems 5 and 6.

5. What was the total number of candy grams sold?

   (A) 26   (B) 27   (C) 25   (D) 28

6. What was the average number of candy grams sold by each person?

   (A) 2   (B) 3   (C) 4   (D) 5

Answer Sheet

Test Practice 1 (page 40)	Test Practice 2 (page 41)	Test Practice 3 (page 42)
1. Ⓐ Ⓑ Ⓒ Ⓓ	1. Ⓐ Ⓑ Ⓒ Ⓓ	1. Ⓐ Ⓑ Ⓒ Ⓓ
2. Ⓐ Ⓑ Ⓒ Ⓓ	2. Ⓐ Ⓑ Ⓒ Ⓓ	2. Ⓐ Ⓑ Ⓒ Ⓓ
3. Ⓐ Ⓑ Ⓒ Ⓓ	3. Ⓐ Ⓑ Ⓒ Ⓓ	3. Ⓐ Ⓑ Ⓒ Ⓓ
4. Ⓐ Ⓑ Ⓒ Ⓓ	4. Ⓐ Ⓑ Ⓒ Ⓓ	4. Ⓐ Ⓑ Ⓒ Ⓓ
5. Ⓐ Ⓑ Ⓒ Ⓓ	5. Ⓐ Ⓑ Ⓒ Ⓓ	5. Ⓐ Ⓑ Ⓒ Ⓓ
6. Ⓐ Ⓑ Ⓒ Ⓓ	6. Ⓐ Ⓑ Ⓒ Ⓓ	6. Ⓐ Ⓑ Ⓒ Ⓓ

Test Practice 4 (page 43)	Test Practice 5 (page 44)	Test Practice 6 (page 45)
1. Ⓐ Ⓑ Ⓒ Ⓓ	1. Ⓐ Ⓑ Ⓒ Ⓓ	1. Ⓐ Ⓑ Ⓒ Ⓓ
2. Ⓐ Ⓑ Ⓒ Ⓓ	2. Ⓐ Ⓑ Ⓒ Ⓓ	2. Ⓐ Ⓑ Ⓒ Ⓓ
3. Ⓐ Ⓑ Ⓒ Ⓓ	3. Ⓐ Ⓑ Ⓒ Ⓓ	3. Ⓐ Ⓑ Ⓒ Ⓓ
4. Ⓐ Ⓑ Ⓒ Ⓓ	4. Ⓐ Ⓑ Ⓒ Ⓓ	4. Ⓐ Ⓑ Ⓒ Ⓓ
5. Ⓐ Ⓑ Ⓒ Ⓓ	5. Ⓐ Ⓑ Ⓒ Ⓓ	5. Ⓐ Ⓑ Ⓒ Ⓓ
6. Ⓐ Ⓑ Ⓒ Ⓓ	6. Ⓐ Ⓑ Ⓒ Ⓓ	6. Ⓐ Ⓑ Ⓒ Ⓓ

46   #3314 Practice Makes Perfect: Word Problems (Grade 4)   © Teacher Created Resources, Inc.